THE 10%

PLAN FOR LIFE

THE 10%

PLAN FOR LIFE

By
Ralph Milano

iUniverse, Inc.
New York Bloomington

iUniverse books may be ordered through booksellers or by contacting:

iUniverse
1663 Liberty Drive
Bloomington, IN 47403
www.iuniverse.com
1-800-Authors (1-800-288-4677)

ISBN: 978-1-4502-1054-6 (sc)
ISBN: 978-1-4502-1053-9 (ebook)

Printed in the United States of America

iUniverse rev. date: 01/21/2010

TABLE OF CONTENTS

DEDICATION

This is dedicated to the students at Bridgewater-Raritan Regional High School. They motivated me to give something back by helping them become financially secure and armed with the knowledge needed to protect their financial futures. After all, they are the future of America. I also want to thank Linda Schulte, Writing Center Assistant for the Bridgewater-Raritan Regional High School for her experience. I want to give a special thanks to Kristin Neumann for all of her suggestions she made to help make my book successful.

INTRODUCTION

I started work in 1968 after two years in the army, 16 of those months were overseas. I attended St. Peter's College in Jersey City, NJ at night, earning a B.A. degree. While going to school at night, I was employed at a major fortune 500 company during the day. This is where I found ways to save money through company plans such as: 401 k, pension plans, profit sharing plans, stock and dividend plans. This is when I came up with the idea that you need a plan in life. After studying all of these plans, I came up with the plan for me which I will gladly share with the students of America.

ABOUT THE AUTHOR

Ralph Milano raised 3 daughters and was able to send them to college, purchase cars for them all using the 10% plan. It works. They saved a lot of money not having to pay any college loans or the interest that would normally go along with it. All three girls are very successful in their jobs. Ralph is very proud of their accomplishments.

CHAPTER ONE

The 10% Plan in Action

This is the only financial program you will ever need. Did you ever say to yourself, I wish I knew then what I know now? Well now is your chance to find out. I decided to let you know what I would do if I was 17 again. In this Book I inform you of life experiences I went through and how I would do them again. Of course a different way on some and others leave alone. After 40 years working with large corporations, I decided to retire and become a Substitute teacher. This turned out to be a very rewarding experience. I wanted the students to be successful, not only in school but in life.

I was talking to them about life, and was inspired by their attention and honesty. I would like to tell you a story about a student who inspired me. Whose honesty made me feel great about today's young adults? I was working on a three day assignment at the school, when a student came to me and said she found a \$20 dollar bill in the class room. I took the twenty and told her I will try to find the person who lost the money. I waited three days but no one came forward to claim the money. I was off for two days, and then I was called in for another assignment.

I saw the little girl who gave me the twenty, I smiled, and called her over and told her no one claimed the money, and gave it to her. She gave me the biggest smile I ever saw in my life. I knew that day I wanted to do something more for the Students, so I started talking more about the 10% plan every day. I told the students that they are the future of America, and I want them to be successful in life. As I was talking to them, I notice they were giving me their attention. This was information they never heard before, so I keep on talking. They started taking notes to tell their parents about the plan. So I put this book together to help more students across the country.

You must follow the PLAN without questions, all distractions and situations, have been thought of and are included in the plan. Do not change the plan because you scared. This will work, you will be fine. The first thing you should do is finish high school, go to college and get a job. Start out by taking 10% of your pay and put it directly in the savings account bank. I know when you first start a job you have very little money and 10% would be pennies going into the bank, but you're developing a good habit and you should do this right away. Don't get discouraged.

Eventually when you get into a company they will have a retirement fund called a 401k, put 10% in that plan. Open an account with a discount broker (eg, Charles Schwab, E-Trade). Realize you have the power now. You can do this without any assistance from stock brokers or any financial institutions that offer all kinds of confusing promises.

You can use the internet to open up your own account with a discount broker. Remember you can do this, believe in yourself. If you set your mind you can accomplish anything. With a discount broker you save on commission. Full service Stock brokers charge you for there services these people are sales people and they make money when you buy or sell stock. They will convince you to buy and then they will convince you to sell. They do not care about you. They care about their commission. The only one who cares about you is the person in the mirror.

Here's the plan Start at the beginning; finish high school, go to college and get a job. After you get the job, you immediately put 10% in a savings account, 10% in the 401k with your company. The 401k plan has a choice of funds to choose from and requires you to inform them of your choices. It's always wise to pick more than one fund. This is my suggestion; pick four funds, cash, bonds, and two stock funds. Then tell the plan manager to put 25% in each fund. The 401k plan should give some kind of a company match. Let's assume it's 10% that the company is giving you. This way you're saving 30 % a year. The remaining 80% of your paycheck should go to your checking account. This is your daily living funds. Use this for whatever you need and enjoy yourself. Remember your savings account, this is something that you're going to build up and eventually use the money to invest in buying 5 stocks in companies that you use there products everyday.

Examples:

If you like the IPod when it first came out the stock to purchase was Apple Inc this one product made the stock sky rocket. It went from $20.00 a share and today November 2009 Apple is now over $206 a share.

How do we buy stocks? Open an account with a discount broker of your choice. Look up the symbol on the company and start buying. You are building up your funds every paycheck in your savings account.

Example:

When you save $12,000 dollars you take 1/12 out every month and buy five stocks that you use everyday. You take $1,000 dollars each month and you equally put it into the five stocks that you use their products. You do this every month. Remember you're putting in 10% every paycheck and you're only taking 1/12 out every month. Once you pick your five stocks you never change, these stocks will be with you for the entire plan, THEY are strong companies, remember if you use their products everyday a million people ARE also buying these products and supporting your company's stock.

Example:

Colgate toothpaste ~ how many people do you think brush their teeth with Colgate? Do you think they will be going out of business? We've been talking now about buying shares in five stocks every month for a long period of time.

Now you're probably wondering when to sell? Remember the stocks you're building up are for your future and that of your family. Do not **sell** these stocks right away. You must build them up over time even though you want to take profits do not **sell** be patient. The plan works if you work the plan. When you get married and have children your first priority is to take care of this child. Now you're putting your stocks away for your children's future, it's for your future as well.

There would be some exceptions for selling these stocks, but you need to proceed with caution and remember never to **sell** your stocks for a splurge, it must be a necessity. Examples of necessities would include need money for college education for your children, a down payment on a house, if you get laid off from your job and your medical insurance terminates or any other unforeseen disaster.

Needed money from these big problem items are built into the plan. That's why you never sell these stocks until you need to make one of these major purchases; think BIG ticket items only! The reason you do not sell these stocks right away is because you are building up shares in these companies. These companies pay dividends, based on how many shares you have determine the amount you receive.

The dividends are payable every three months which you should keep in the account. Tell the broker to keep it in the account so you can buy more shares later. Every paycheck you put in 10% in your account along with the dividends will build up your account fast.

Another way of getting more shares is when the stock splits. This is how this works, if you have 500 hundred shares of Apple Inc at $20 a share, and the company announces a stock split, you will now have 1000 shares at $10 a share. It is the same amount of money but you have more shares at half price and remember that dividend. The reason for stock splits is the company is trying to get people to buy the stock at a lower price, so they can sell more shares. That drives the stock price higher; you have to hold onto the stock for a longer period of time. So your shares may go to $20 again and now you have doubled your money.

An example is Apple Inc. If you were to invest $10,000 at $20 a share you would've had 500 shares. Apple split four times that would've given you in your account 8,000 shares today at $200 a share, your account would be worth 1.6 million. The reason for this large amount is because you did not sell your shares. You were patient, you were tempted, but you stuck to the plan because you are disciplined. You don't have fear, because you have the plan!

Ralph's Picks

These are my choices for 5 stocks and the reasons I pick them. Please remember that you are to pick stocks that you use their products, but if you like these then use them for your plan.

1. **General Mills, Inc**. (Symbol=GIS) 70.95
   Dividend $1.96 [2.80%] General Mills. Inc

engages in the manufacture and marketing of branded consumer foods worldwide. The company also supplies branded and unbranded food products to the foodservice and commercial baking industries.

2. **Colgate Palmolive** (Symbol=CL) 83.15 Dividend $1.76 [2.10%] Colgate-Palmolive Company, together with its subsidiaries, manufactures and markets consumer products worldwide. It operates in two segments, Oral, Personal, and Home Care; and Pet Nutrition.

3. **Kellogg Co**. (Symbol=K) 54.00 Dividend $1.50 [2.80%] Kellogg Company, together with its subsidiaries, engages in the manufacture and marketing of ready-to-eat cereal and convenience foods. Its principal products include ready-to-eat cereals and convenience foods such as cookies and crackers.

4. **Sysco Corp.** (Symbol=SYY) 28.53 Dividend $.96 [3.40%] Sysco Corporation, through its subsidiaries, markets and distributes a range of food and related products primarily to the foodservice industry in the United States.

5. **Merck & Co Inc**. (Symbol=MRK) 36.99 Dividend $1.52 [4.10%] Merck & Co Inc. provides products for human and animal health primarily in the United States. The company's Pharmaceutical segment offers human health pharmaceutical products, such as therapeutic and preventive agents.

The prices of these stocks are from the closing bell on December, 24 2009. Sometimes you will come across a company that makes more than one product that you use, that is the one you will choose. Most of the good company's make many products. Pick the company that makes the products you use most or more than one, also look for that high dividend.

Remember only trust the person in the mirror.

CHAPTER TWO

A Plan for Every Age

It should be clearly noted that the plan can be used by any age. Seventeen is the starting point. You will have disciplined and developing a good habit in savings. You can't buy stocks until you are 21 so from 17 to 21 you save in the bank. At 21 you start purchasing the 5 stocks, remember these are the companies you use there products. Take 1/12th out of the savings account every month, it should be clearly noted that you should buy 100 shares of a stock because you would receive a discount for not breaking up the block.

At 30 years old if you want to start the plan its fine. You should have a savings account set up so all you have to do is put 10% every pay in the account. You can start buying the 5 stocks right away. Remember buy 100 share blocks and take 1/12th out every month and never sell the shares until you have a real need. If you have enough money in the bank you might want to buy more than 100 shares of each stock because you started late that's ok to do, just keep putting 10% every pay in the bank. At 40 years old follow the same plan but at this age you have to be aware of Investment Scams. Ponzi scams that promise huge returns. Financial advisors who prey on widows and widowers be careful of anyone who contacts you offering to help you with your finances soon after your spouse dies.

These are unethical people looking to take advantage in others during this emotional time. Watch out for high yield investments scams, unscrupulous advisers are peddling products that have the highest yield and promising you safety of your investments that just isn't true. When you are at the 60 age group you have to watch out for Scams that want you to pay up front. Example Prepaid Funeral. A funeral can be one of the most expensive purchases you will ever make. A typical funeral costs about $6000, but costs can go as high as $10,000. To spare your family from expenses and decisions making during this emotional time, a growing number of people are pre-paying their funeral expenses.

The idea is that you pre-pay for your funeral and those funds are held in escrow, in a trust or used to buy life insurance that would cover funeral expenses when you die. But pre-paid funeral scams swindle millions of dollars each year. In the worst scams, people take your money and simply get sold an expensive package that costs much more than you need to spend. The last thing grieving relatives need is to find out you were ripped off and there is a large unexpected funeral expense with which to deal.

Let the plan pay for all your final expenses. Do not give anyone upfront money.

Another Scam at this age is Fake E mails from Social Security Administration. There are many variations of these fake messages circulating, but they all claim there is something wrong with your Social Security benefits and that convince you to click the link provided to clear up the problem. Here's a sample. Due to possible calculation errors, your annual Social Security statement may contain errors. Use the link below to review your annual Social Security statement.

The scammers have done a good job making these e-mails look legitimate. They use a gov e-mail address as all government sites use. Some messages even contain the Social Security Administration logo, making them look very official. Don't fall for it! These e-mails are not from the Social Security Administration. Their sole purpose, as with most e-mail scams, is to trick you into sharing important information that will help the scammer steal your identity, access your bank account or otherwise cause you financial harm.

The Social Security Administration does NOT contact consumers through e-mail, period. What you should do is not open the e-mail. You only have to work the Plan and assign a family member to handle the arrangements for your funeral with the Plan money. You should only need $6000 to $8000 and you will not get ripped off. Your family will thank you for being thoughtful at this trying time.

What Is Social Security? Social Security primarily refers social welfare service concerned with social protection, or protection against socially recognized conditions, including poverty, old age, disability, unemployment and others. Although some publications use the terms [social security and social protection] interchangeably, social security is used both more narrowly [to refer only to schemes with the formal title of social security] and more widely [referring to many kinds of social welfare scheme]. Social Security may refer to:

Social insurance, where people receive benefits or services in recognition of contributions to an insurance scheme.

These services typically include provision for retirement, pension's disability insurance, survivor benefits and unemployment. Income Maintenance, mainly the distribution of cash in the event of interruption of employment, including retirement, disability and unemployment. Services – provided by administrations responsible for social security.

Social Security is a PLAN. It's like the 401k plan I talk about in chapter one Let's look at the social security plan, the government takes money out of your check and puts it in an account for you. The company you work for must match it 100%. You can not touch this money until retirement, that begins at 62 or you can wait for a later age 65 or 66 and receive a larger amount. The 401k plan is when you put money in your account according to the rules of the plan and the company will add a % depending on the employer.

You do not have to join the 401k plan but if you do not you will be giving up some free money. This plan requires that you keep the money in the plan until you reach 59-1/2 years old. If you want to take money out early you will pay a 10% penalty. Both plans are good for you if you follow the rules. Now you are ready to work your retirement, with the Plan, the 401k and social security. Remember the plan you are buying stocks every month, so this requires you to do homework. The other two plans are automatic after you get a job.

Remember only trust the person in the mirror.

CHAPTER THREE

Stock Market

In the plan I tell you to buy 5 stocks, these are companies you are using the Products they make. Now it's time to tell you how the stock market works.

The stock market appears in the news everyday. You hear about it any time it reaches a new high or a new low, and you also hear about it daily in statements like the Dow Jones Industrial average rose today.

Obviously, stocks and the stock market are important, but you may find that you know very little about them. What is a stock? What is a stock market? Why do we need a stock market? Where does the stock come from to begin with, and why do people want to buy and sell it? If you have questions like these then this will open your eyes to a whole new world! Determining value, let's say that you want to start a business, and you decide to open a restaurant. You go out and buy a building, buy all the kitchen equipment, tables and chairs that you need, buy your supplies and hire your cooks, servers, ect. You advertise and open the doors. Let's say that you spend $500,000 buying the building and the equipment.

In the first year, you spend $250,000 on supplies, food and the payroll for your employees. At the end of the first year, you add up all the money you have received from customers and find that your total income is $300,000. Since you made $300,000 and out the $250,000 for expenses, your net profit $50,000. At the end of the second year, you bring in $325,000 and your expenses remain the same, for a net profit of $75,000. At this point, you decide that you want to sell the business. What is it worth? One way to look at it is to say that the business is worth $500,000. If you close the restaurant, you can sell the building, the equipment and everything else and get $500,000. This is a simplification, of course the building probably went up in value, and the equipment went down because it is now used.

Let's just say that things balance out to $500,000. This is the asset value, of the business the value of all of the business's assets if you sold them outright today. But what if you keep it going? If you keep the restaurant going, it will probably make at lease $75,000 this year you know that from your history with the business. Therefore, you can think of the restaurant as an investment that will pay something like $75,000 in interest every year. Looking at it that way, someone might be willing to pay $750,000 for the restaurant, as a $75,000 return per year on a $750,000 investment represents a 10 percent rate of return. Someone might even be willing to pay $1,500,000, which represents a 5 percent rate of return or more if, he or she though that the restaurant's income would grow and increase earnings over time at a rate faster than the rate of inflation.

The restaurant's owner, therefore, will set the price accordingly; you might price the restaurant at $1,500,000. What if 10 people come to you and say, wow, I would like to buy your restaurant but I don't have $1,500,000. You might want to somehow divide your restaurant into 10 equal pieces and sell each piece for $150,000. In other words, you might sell shares in the restaurant. Then, each person who bought a share would receive one tenth of the profits at the end of the year, and each person would have one out of 10 votes in any business decisions. Or, you might divide ownership up into 1,500 shares and sell each share for $1,000 to make the price something that more people could afford. Or you might divide ownership up into 3,000 shares, keep 1,500 for yourself, and sell the remaining shares for $500 each. That way, you retain a majority of the shares and therefore the votes and remain in control of the restaurant while sharing the profit with other people.

In the meantime, you get to put $750,000 in the bank when you sell the 1,500 shares to other people. Stock, at its core, is really that simple. It represents ownership of a company's assets and profits. A dividend on a share of stock represents that share's portion of the company's profits, generally dispersed yearly. If the restaurant has 10 owners, each owning one share of stock and the restaurant makes $75,000 in profit during the year, and then each owner gets a dividend of $7,500. A large company like IBM has millions of shares of stock outstanding. In this case, the total profits of the company are divided and sent to the shareholders as dividends.

Stocks in publicly traded companies are bought and sold at a stock market.

The New York Stock Exchange is an example of such a market. In your neighborhood, you have a supermarket that sells food. The reason you go to the supermarket is because you can go to one place and buy all of the different types of food that you need in one stop it's a lot more convenient than driving around to the butcher, the dairy farmer, the baker, ect. The NYSE is a supermarket for stocks. The NYSE can be thought of as a big room where everyone who wants to buy and sell shares of stocks can go to do their buying and selling.

The exchange makes buying and selling easy. You don't have to actually travel to New York to visit the New York Stock Exchange you can call a stock broker who does business with the NYSE, and he or she will go to the NYSE on your behalf to buy or sell your stock. If the exchange did not exist, buying or selling stock would be a lot harder. You would have to place a classified ad in the newspaper, wait for a call and haggle on a price whenever you wanted to sell stock. With an exchange in place, you can buy and sell shares instantly.

The stock exchange has an interesting side effect. Because all the buying and selling is concentrated in one place, it allows the price of a stock to be known every second of the day. Therefore, investors can watch as a stock's price fluctuates based on news from the company, media reports, national economic news and lots of other factors. Buyers and sellers take all of these factors into account. Investors could not be sure that the airline represented a going concern and began selling, driving the price down. The asset value of the company acted as a floor on the share price. The price of a stock also reflects the dividend that the stock pays the projected earnings of the company in the future.

Any business that wants to sell shares of stock to a number of different people does so by turning itself into a Corporation. The process of turning a business into a corporation is called incorporating.

If you start a restaurant by taking your own money to buy the building and the equipment, then what you have done is formed a sole proprietorship. You own the entire restaurant yourself you get to make all of the decisions and you keep all of the profit. If three people pool their money together and start a restaurant as a team, what they have done is formed a partnership. The three people own the restaurant themselves, sharing the profit and decision making.

A corporation is different, and it is a pretty interesting concept. A corporation is a virtual person. That is, a corporation is registered with the government, it has a social security number, it can own property, it can go to court to sue people, it can be sued and it can make contracts. By definition, a corporation has stock that can be bough and sold, and all of the owners of the corporation hold shares of stock in the corporation to represent their ownership. One incredibly interesting characteristic of this virtual person is that it has an indefinite and potentially infinite life span.

There is a whole body of law that controls corporations these laws are in place to protect the shareholders and the public. These laws control a number of things about how a corporation operates and is organized. For example, every corporation has a board of directors if all of the shares of a corporation are owned by one person, then that one person can decide that there will only be one person on the board of directors, but there is still a board. The shareholders in the company meet every year to vote on the people for the board.

The board of directors makes the decisions for the company. It hires the officers the president and other major officers of the company, makes the company's decisions and sets the company's policies. The board of directors can be thought of as the brain of the virtual person.

Shareholders, from this description, you can see that a corporation has a group of owners the shareholders. The owners elect a board of directors to make the company's major decisions. The owners of a corporation become owners by buying shares of stock in the corporation. The board of directors decides how many total shares there will be. For example, a company might have one million shares of stock. The company can either be privately held or publicly held. In a privately held company, the shares of stock are owned by a small number of people who probably all know one another. They buy and sell their shares amongst themselves. A publicly held company is owned by thousands of people who trade their shares on a public stock exchange.

One of the big reasons why corporations exist is to create a structure for collecting lots of investment dollars in a business. Let's say that you would like to start your own airline. Most people cannot do this, because an airline costs millions of dollars. An airline needs a whole fleet of planes and other equipment, plus it has to hire a lot of employees. A person who wants to start an airline will therefore form a corporation and sell stock in order to collect the money needed to get started.

A corporation is an easy way to gather large quantities of investment capital money from investors. When a corporation first sells stock to the public, it does so in an Initial Public Offering.

The company might sell one million shares of stock at $20 a share to raise $20 million very quickly that is a simplification the brokerage house in charge of the IPO will extract its fee from the $20 million. The company then invests the $20 million in equipment and employees. The investors the shareholders who bought the $20 million in stock hope that with the equipment and employees, the company will make a profit and pay a dividend.

Another reason that corporations exist is to limit liability of the owners to some extent. If the corporation gets sued, it is the corporation that pays the settlement. The corporation may go out of business, but that is the worst that can happen. If you are a sole proprietor who owns a restaurant and the restaurant gets sued, you are the one who is being sued. You and the restaurant are the same thing. If you lose the suit then you, personally, can lose everything you own in the process.

Stock Prices, Let's say that a new corporation is created and in its IPO it raises $20 million by selling one million shares at $20 a share.

The corporation buys its equipment and hires its employees with that money. In the first year, when all the income and expenses are added up, the company makes a profit of $1 million. The board of directors of the company can decide to do a number of things with that $1 million. It could put it in the bank and save it for a rainy day. It could decide to give all of the profits to the shareholders, so it would declare a dividend of $1 per share. It could use the money to buy more equipment and hire more employees to expand the company. It could pick some combination of these three options. If a company traditionally pays out most its profits to its shareholders, it is generally called an income stock. The shareholders get income from the company's profits. If the company puts most of the money back into the business, it is called a growth stock. The company is trying to grow larger by increasing the amount of equipment and the number of people who run it. Income vs. Growth The price of an income stock tends to stay fairly flat. That is, from year to year, the price of the stock tends to remain about the same unless profits and therefore dividends go up.

People are getting their money each year and the business is not growing. This would be the case for stock in a single restaurant that distributes all of its profits to the shareholders each year. Let's say that the single restaurant decides, for several years, to save its profits, and eventually it opens a second restaurant. That is the behavior of a growth company.

The value of the stocks rises because, when the second restaurant opens there is twice as much equipment and twice as much profit being earned by the company. In a growth stock, the shareholders do not get a yearly dividend, but they own a company whose value is increasing. Therefore, the shareholders can get more money when they sell their shares someone buying the stock would see the increasing book value of the company the value of the buildings, equipment, etc. and the increasing profit that the company is earning and, based on these factors, pay a higher price for the stock.

Remember only trust the person in the mirror.

CHAPTER FOUR

Stock Options

Job ads in the classifieds mention stock options more and more frequently. Companies are offering these benefit not just too top executives but also to rank and file employees. What are stock options? Why are companies offering them? Are employees guaranteed a profit just because they have stock options? The answer to these questions will give a much better idea about this increasingly popular movement. Let's start with a simple definition of stock options.

Stock Options from your employer give you the right to buy a specific number of shares of your company's stock during a time and at a price that your employer specifies. Both privately and publicly held companies make options available for several reasons. They want to attract and keep good workers. They want their employees to feel like owners or partners in the business. They want to hire skilled workers by offering compensation that goes beyond a salary. This is especially true in start up companies that want to hold on to as much cash as possible. Benefits of stock options the employees can exercise the price the company sets on the stock is discounted and is usually the market price of the stock at the time the employee is given the option.

Since those options cannot be exercised for some time, the hope is that the price of the shares will go up so that selling them later at a higher market price will yield a profit. You can see, then, that unless the company goes out of business or doesn't perform well, offering stock options is a good way to motivate workers to accept jobs and stay on. Those stock options promise potential cash or stock in addition to salary. Let's look at a real world example to help you understand how this might work. Say company x gives or grants its employees options to buy 100 shares of stock at $5 a share. Keeps the option starting Aug 1; 2009.On Aug.

1, 2009, the stock is at $10. Here are the choices for the employee.

The first thing an employee can do is convert the option to stock, buy it at $5 a share, then turn around and sell all the stock after a waiting period specified in the options contract. If an employee sells those 100 shares, that's a gain of $5 a share, or $500 in profit. Another thing an employee can do is sell some of the stock after the waiting period and keep some to sell later. Again, the employee has to buy the stock at $5 a share first.

The last choice is to change all the options to stock, buy it at the discounted price and it with the idea of selling it later, maybe when each share is worth $15. Whatever choice an employee makes, though, the options have to be converted to stock, which brings us to another aspect of stock options, the vesting period.

In the example with Company x, employees could exercise their options and buy all 100 shares at once if they wanted to. Usually, though, a company will spread out the vesting period, maybe over three or five or 10 years, and let employees buy so many shares according to a schedule. Here's how that might work. You get options on 100 shares of stock in your company. The vesting schedule for your options is spread out over four years, with one-fourth vested the first year, one-fourth vested the second, one-fourth vested the third, and one-fourth vested the fourth year. This means you can buy 25 shares at the grant or strike price the first year, then 25 shares each year after until you're fully vested in the fourth year.

Remember that each year you can buy 25 shares of stock at a discount, then keep it or sell it at the current market value. And each year you're going to hope the stock price continues to rise another thing to know about options is that they always have an expiration date. You can exercise your options starting on a certain date and ending on a certain date. If you don't exercise the option within that period, you lose them. And if you are leaving a company, you can only exercise your vested options, you will lose any future vesting.

Overall, you can see that stock options do have risk, and they are not always better than cash compensation if the company is not successful, but they are becoming a built-in feature in many industries.

Remember only trust the person in the mirror.

CHAPTER FIVE

Scams on the Internet & TV

We all like to buy items on the internet. It's very convenient for shopping and it gives you a sense of security, but we have to be aware of what people are doing with your personal information. Be careful using your credit card when you purchase items on the internet. Your personal information is being stored by companies and being sold to many other companies. When you purchase something for $19.95 there is an additional cost for shipping and handling in the fine print which can range from $6 to $7 per item. This is where the company makes their money.

The $19.95 is a luring price to get you to order, you may even get two items for the price of one. All you need to pay is for the shipping and handling. You should be aware that this is a marked up price for the shipping and handling and the company is making a huge profit from the outrageous costs of shipping and handling.

If you want to know what the legitimate costs for shipping and handling for the package that you just received go to the local post office and weigh and ask them to give you the cost of what a first class or third class mailing rate would be. You should ask yourself a question is why is everything $19.95? Why are they willing to double the product for the same price?

My suggestion is to purchase one of these pre-paid Visa cards from your local store and use it when you purchase on the internet. This way you are not giving out your personal information. This is the best way to avoid identity theft. I know the urge exists to purchase on the internet, these ads are very convincing. My point is here, you are buying something for $19.95 but the whole underlying purpose behind the sale is to gather information about you.

It should be clearly noted that as soon as your purchase something on the internet that you'll be receiving 100 e mails a day on your e mail from other companies trying to sell you their items because you are on their list. The more you click on those advertisement e mails, the more junk you will receive, like it or not.

Remember these items are all low priced and probably will not last too long. You are aware of the shipping and handling are built in and marked. The safest thing to do is to use the pre-paid Visa card, if you have to purchase things on the internet. You it will only cost you $25.00 for the purchase of this card and a small fee of $3.00 and you get the security and peace of mind of protecting yourself from loosing your identity.

The best places to buy products on the internet are from stores you are familiar with and are located in your local malls. This way if you have a problem you can go to the store directly and meet with someone face to face and discuss your situation, this will make your shopping much easier and dependable.

Watch out for the checking your credit scores for free on TV or the internet. They will ask for all of your personal information. My main question is how can they advertise that it's for free when they're asking you for a credit card? They say it's only $1.00, then why do they say free score. com? They want your credit card. Within seven days you will receive a charge on your credit card for $12.95 for their services monitoring your credit activity. None of which you asked for. They are selling your information without your consent to other companies so they can contact you to buy their products.

This should serve as a wake up call to avoid that web site. If you really want to know your credit score just go to your local automotive dealer and tell them you're interested in purchasing or leasing a vehicle and they will be happy to run your credit report to see if you're qualified. This has a twofold purpose one to see if you're qualified and the other to actually get your credit report.

One of the main complaints I have about TV ads is that they use well known celebrities to endorse their products. Why do they do that? I'll tell you why because you like that person as a celebrity and you become familiar with them and you have a Hard time believing that they would mislead or lie to you. They are wealthy and can buy any product they want and if they can do it then I'll trust in that person too. What is the reason the celebrity does this? Money, easy money! The celebrity reads a dummy card and gets a check from the company, but guess who the real dummy is if you fall for it? You! Remember that the celebrity is not really involved in the decision making of the product and is not aware of the defects that could cause the product to be recalled.

Their sole purpose is to receive a check. I feel that the celebrity has a responsibility not to do commercials that are misleading because people are buying a product because of their celebrity status. And we all know that they do not need the situation. Why does a person that makes 20 million a year need to do a commercial for more money?

The word is just simply Greed! Instead, he should be thinking about the true consequences of his actions instead of the paycheck. My advice to you is to watch your favorite player on TV buy his t-shirt have it signed and enjoy the game and as soon as you see his advertising something change the channel he is just a puppet for the corporation to try and get you to buy something. If you want to buy a car I'll give you a technique without listening to a celebrity on TV. First find out the kind of car you want, lets say you want a Honda Civic, so you go to a Honda Dealer closest to you and you tell them you want to lease a Civic whatever the standard equipment it comes with. Tell them you have no money, no trade in, you just want to sign and drive. He will give you a price for a sign and drive. Then you go to another Honda dealer in another town do the same thing. Then go to another dealer in another town and do the same thing. Three different towns, you write down the price for each one.

It's very simple you know what the cheapest price is for the same standard car. There is nothing he can do to change the price. Now that you have the price which one are you going to go back to lease or purchase the car? Now you make your deal he's the lowest one and the most honest one out of the three dealers. Now you can talk to him about any other additions that you'd like to make. I personally do not like to trade in cars to dealers you never get a good price. What I would do is donate your car to charity where you will get a complete write off on your taxes.

Another strategy that I'd like to use is to tell them that you'll buy the car under one condition, tell them to eliminate the donut tire in the trunk and replace it with a full size tire. Believe me they will not want to loose a sale over a tire; before you get to the door they'll call you back.

Another strategy is for an item that you want to buy for your home is calling the vendor in and ask them to show you an installation that he's made in the neighborhood. Have him make an appointment to go to that person's house to see his work. Two things should happen the vendor should be happy to show off his work and the people should recommend him for the job based on what you've seen. If you like what he did in their home and they recommend him, go with that vendor. Remember the best advertising is a satisfied customer. That's what you did you found a satisfied customer and you saw the finished product, this is all you need to make the right decision.

Remember only trust the person in the mirror.

CHAPTER SIX

Insurance & Credit Cards

Growing areas of the insurance industry are medical services and health insurance, and its expansion into other financial services, such as securities and mutual funds.

Jobs in office and administrative occupations usually may be entered with a high school diploma, but employers prefer college graduates for sales, managerial, and professional jobs.

The insurance industry provides protection against financial losses resulting from a variety of hazards. By purchasing insurance policies, individuals and businesses can receive reimbursement for losses due to car accidents, theft of property, and fire and storm damage; medical expenses; and loss of income due to disability or death.

The insurance industry consists mainly of insurance carriers and insurance agencies and brokerages. In general, insurance carriers are large companies that provide insurance and assume the risks covered by the policy. Insurance agencies and brokerages sell insurance policies for the carriers. While some of agencies and brokerages are directly affiliated with a particular carrier and sell only that carrier's policies, many are independent and are thus free to market the policies of a variety of insurance carriers.

In addition to these two primary components, the insurance industry includes establishments that provide other insurance-related services, such as claims adjustment or third-party administration of insurance and pension funds. These other insurance industry establishments also include a number of independent organizations that provide a wide array of insurance-related services to carriers and their clients. One such service is the processing of claims forms for medical practitioners. Other services include loss prevention and risk management. Also, insurance companies sometimes hire independent claims adjusters to investigate accidents and claims for property damage and to assign a dollar estimate to the claim.

Insurance carriers assume the risk associated with annuities and insurance policies and assign premiums to be paid for the policies. In the policy, the carrier states the length and conditions of the agreement, exactly which losses it will provide compensation for, and how much will be awarded. The premium charged for the policy is based primarily on the amount to be awarded in case of loss and the likelihood that the insurance carrier will actually have to pay.

In order to be able to compensate policyholders for their losses, insurance companies invest the money they receive in premiums, building up a portfolio of financial assets and income-producing real estate which can then be used to pay off any future claims that may be brought. There are two basic types of insurance carriers. Primary carriers are responsible for the initial underwriting of insurance policies and annuities, while reinsurance carriers assume all or part of the risk associated with the existing insurance policies originally underwritten by other insurance carriers.

Primary insurance carriers offer a variety of insurance policies. Life insurance provides financial protection to beneficiaries—usually spouses and dependent children—upon the death of the insured. Disability insurance supplies a preset income to an insured person who is unable to work due to injury or illness, and health insurance pays the expenses resulting from accidents and illness.

An annuity (a contract or a group of contracts that furnishes a periodic income at regular intervals for a specified period) provides a steady income during retirement for the remainder of one's life. Property-casualty insurance protects against loss or damage to property resulting from hazards such as fire, theft, and natural disasters. Liability insurance protects policyholders from financial responsibility for injuries to others or for damage to other people's property. Most policies, such as automobile and homeowner's insurance, combine both property-casualty and liability coverage. Companies that underwrite this kind of insurance are called property-casualty carriers.

Some insurance policies cover groups of people, ranging from a few to thousands of individuals. These policies usually are issued to employers for the benefit of their employees or to unions, professional associations, or other membership organizations for the benefit of their members. Among the most common policies of this nature are group life and health plans. Insurance carriers also underwrite a variety of specialized types of insurance, such as real-estate title insurance, employee safety and fidelity bonding, and medical malpractice insurance.

Other organizations in the industry are formed by groups of insurance companies, to perform functions that would result in a duplication of effort if each company carried them out individually. For example, service organizations are supported by insurance companies to provide loss statistics, which the companies use to set their rates.

The recent financial crisis has resulted in large losses for the insurance industry. Industry conditions in the near term remain tenuous, particularly as many companies will continue to experience declining revenues, investment losses, and credit rating downgrades, which can affect an insurer's ability to repay debt by having to pay a higher interest rate. Additionally, insurance companies who were trading in credit default swaps and other risky instruments without sufficient hedging suffered especially hard, and some companies even became insolvent. Companies with prudent risk management strategies also suffered large losses, because most investment instruments owned by insurance companies experienced falling values as they were being sold or marked down as the stock market deteriorated in late 2008. Nonetheless, as insurers rebuild capital and adhere to stricter Federal regulations, the insurance industry is likely to stabilize.

Insurance carriers now sell products traditionally associated with other financial institutions, such as banks and securities firms. These products include securities, mutual funds, and various retirement plans.

The Internet is an important tool for insurance carriers in reaching potential and existing customers. Carriers use the Internet to enable customers to access online account and billing information, submit claims, view insurance quotes, and purchase policies. In addition to individual carrier-sponsored Internet sites, several "lead-generating" sites have emerged. These sites allow potential customers to input information about their insurance policy needs. For a fee, the sites forward customer information to a number of insurance companies, which review the information and, if they decide to take on the policy, contact the customer with an offer. This practice gives consumers the freedom to accept the best rate.

The best advertising is a satisfied customer. Trust only the person in the mirror. You've heard these statements before in the other chapters. In this chapter I want you to trust your parents because when you're 17 years old you need to buy a car and get your driver's license. The law requires you to have car insurance. The best way to obtain car insurance is to be added onto your parent's policy. This is the cheapest and easiest way to get insurance.

I want you to be there when your father calls the insurance man over because you're going to ask some questions for your future insurance needs. Some of the questions should be: Does your company cover homeowner's life/health insurance? Because in order to get a mortgage you're going to need to get homeowner's insurance.

My point is that you are not going to need all of these now, but you will in the future and the only way to beat the insurance company is to give them all of your insurance needs this will help you get an edge because if anything happens with any of your policies they will work with you to keep you insured with them.

If you just had one type of insurance policy and you had an auto accident, then you could be dropped, but this assures you that you will not be dropped since you are showing loyalty to them by having other insurance policies. The company is the most important part of your decision making not the agent. If the agent leaves his company do not follow the agent. They will want you to because he or she wants to keep your business. Your loyalty lays with the actual company not the agent. The company is an asset to you, and your loyalty will buy you additional discounts for multiple policies.

Do not pick a company because of clever adverting jingles. Pick a company that has multiple policies that you can benefit from. Car insurance is something you need because of the law; insurance is something you need because you can not obtain a mortgage without one. Other insurances that are very popular when you have children are term life insurance on you because if something happens to you when your children are young this is a very good type of policy that will protect them. Usually it's a large amount like $500,000 to a million dollars. Now this is called term insurance because you have a specific number of years before the policy expires.

You can work with the agent on the term years. When your children are 21 they will be on their own, your term insurance will be worth zero after 20 years. You gave the insurance 20 years of good premiums and this was for protection of your children and you received a piece of mind. This is what you are paying for. The insurance company is planning on you living and you are planning on dying because if you die then your children will receive a big lump sum to take care of them for the rest of their lives. You brought these children into the world and it's your responsibility to protect them until they are old enough to take care of themselves. Now you have your car and you're on your parent's insurance policy.

The next thing you need is a credit card so you can establish your own credit. Things a credit card user should know. Even if you make your credit card payments on time, the credit card bank can raise your interest rate automatically if you're late on payments elsewhere, such as on another credit card, or on a phone, car, or house payment or simply because the bank feels you have taken on too much debt.

The best way to get good credit is to go to a department store like Macys and fill out an application for their credit card. The first time you make a purchase with that credit card you will receive a 10% discount on that item. What I'd like you to do is to use that credit card and pay off that bill in thirty days. Then I'd like you to do this again every month for the next six months. Only the initial purchase you make you'll receive the 10 % however you will be establishing a credit history for yourself. You must complete the six months of payment with your Macy's card; the next application you should fill out is for a Visa card. Try to purchase a Visa card that offers you a reward program. Remember that you must pay entire bill by the due date. I like the Visa Travel Continental Card. I use Continental for the frequent flyer miles which I use to upgrade from coach to first class. When you have their card they tend to give you a more VIP service. There are Visa cards that offer you other reward programs. Pick out the one that suits you best and apply for it. It is important to know that you really do not need many credit cards. One department store card and one Visa card is plenty for you to establish good credit.

Please do not get more than two, you run the risk of loosing cards and having your identity stolen. Your credit score known as a FICO score has become a vital statistic for many Americans and can be widely shared. It is used to determine how much you can borrow, how much you pay for life insurance, if you can rent a home, and, as already noted, it can be a factor in determining the interest rate you pay on a credit card. It's important to read the fine print in your credit card agreement. Not many people do, however, even credit card executives and consumer advocates admitted that the last time they read their own contracts was years ago and the credit card agreement is difficult to understand.

Tucked into the fine print that people so often ignore is a clause that allows the company to change your interest rate at any time, for any reason, as long as they give you 15 days' notice. If they do this to you get mad, call them up and tell them you are looking at another credit card company that will treat you better. This sometimes helps, especially if you're a good customer.

Remember only trust the person in the mirror.

CHAPTER SEVEN

Politics

Daddy, take me to the Bank

The following is my opinion on how to help the American people with a stimulus package, and other programs.

Eliminate the Penny — The government should stop making pennies and make every penny out there be worth a nickel. This gives the people five times their money, but the rule is that they have to bring their pennies to the bank. Open up a new account or deposit them in an existing account. Follow all bank rules for depositing pennies of course. The bank would then give the pennies back to the government and the government would issue them a check for all the pennies they turned in. This would be an easy transaction because everyone's account would grow. What is the benefit for the people? They would get five cents for every penny. The bank would receive more money in their bank. The bank would want this to grow the business.

The government would not have the production costs of making the penny. Transactions in the stores would be much easier. I'm sure that there might be situations that stores do not convert their computers for this change so we would go with a very simple solution for example a $1.03 would then become a $1.05 a $1.02 would be a $1.00. The penny will now be even more valuable and desirable as people cash them in for 5 cents each at there local bank. Maybe the government could melt the pennies down for defense or products for housing.

Medicare — My suggestion is that the government should pay100%. On all claims, and allow seniors to start signing up for Medicare at age 62. This would help by giving people age 62 full coverage for medical insurance. Maybe this would give the people at age 62 an incentive to leave their jobs. This would allow more jobs to open up and give SOME opportunities to the unemployed Americans.

We have to stop the scams that are going on with Medicare. I would suggest that people that are 62 and older to verify the bill before the government pays. There are plenty of phony bills that are being submitted and the Medicare participant does not even get a chance to correct the bill.

We need their assistance to verify that the bill is correct and that services performed were satisfactory. This gives the Medicare Members a little more authority over their doctor because they have to verify the bill in order for the doctor to get paid. This also gives the Medicare member the opportunity to go to any doctor in the United States. They do not need to be limited to picking a doctor out of a book. There will be no more books for Medicare members. You go to the doctor you want.

The doctors should be happy with this plan because it's backed up 100% by the government for reimbursement. How do we pay for this? Very simple, do not give HMO's any more money for Medicare; and Stop Medicare Fraud. Medicare users are a favorite scam target. Some scammers offer seniors free medical products all they have to do is give them their Medicare number. Another common ploy is to tell a senior that their Medicare card has expired and they need to provide their Medicare number to get a new one. They just want to steal your number so they can scam Medicare out of more money. If we take care of our Senior Americans we're taking care of our country.

Flat Tax — I worked for a large corporation for fourteen years and they came up with a bonus plan for all employees, it was a 15% maximum profit sharing plan. This was very simple to understand. The bonus would include 15% of your salary every year. You had the opportunity to leave it in the company cash plan or move it into the company stock.

The point I'm trying to make here is that everyone received 15% of their salary so the higher the salary the higher the bonus. No one complained everyone understood the plan. I feel that our current income tax is broken down into two many brackets. If we had a flat tax based on your salary then everyone would pay a 15% flat tax. It would come out of your pay paycheck and you wouldn't have to worry about filling out your income taxes every year.

There would be no "loopholes" or deductions. That is your portion of taxes and the government would receive it every week. There would be no need for IRS forms or deductions anymore. It should be clearly noted that if anyone on unemployment or Medicare, shouldn't be paying any taxes at all until they get a job. The system should also include $100 of food stamps every week while you are looking for a job. Why is welfare only getting food stamps? When you're unemployed you need to feel that you're getting help from the system and people care at the unemployment office. I believe people really want to work, and be part of society. If we make people feel good, they will be successful on their interviews for the job.

Companies should get a tax credit for hiring the unemployed. I also recommend companies should be fined when they lay off employees at 55, when it's very clear they just want to avoid paying benefits. Companies need to be more understanding with the market conditions. It is much easier for a 25 year old to find a new job than a 55 year old. People at 55 have a very hard time to recover and most of the time they get sick or divorced, and run into credit problems.

The Human Resources dept at the company should be more protective to employees at age 55 and older. Many big HR depts., in insurance companies, banks, and the like, consciously recruit from the lower half of the barrel to save money. If they only realized what they were doing to themselves, it would be a better company. The trouble with HR experts is that they use gimmicks borrowed from manufacturing. This manufacturing of men is not effective, it's destructive. HUMAN RESOURCES should provide the climate and proper nourishment and let the people grow themselves.

The flat tax would be very hard to say it's unfair because you would be taxed 15% of your salary. The more money you make the more taxes you should pay and you should be happy you're paying more taxes because you're making more money. I'm not sure of all of the savings the government would have by not using these forms, with the high costs of printing and mailings, but there would be a definite savings for the American Public because there would not be any penalties or late fees; it would come out of their check every time they get paid. It should be clearly noted that your refund check is not a gift from the government, it's your money you over paid. When you get back it will be with out interest.

Remember only trust the person in the mirror.

CHAPTER EIGHT

Conclusion

It is important to know that this is a plan that works. I want you to follow it. Put 10 % of your paycheck in a savings account. Put 10 % in a 401 K and the company will match or give some %. It will work if you give it the time to make it happen. Remember you are starting out you have to use this plan when you are 17 years old. I know you don't make a lot of money but you are developing a good habit for savings. When you start seeing the money grow, and this might take 6 years then you'll be ready to buy stocks.

You know I mentioned in the first chapter that you have to buy stocks from the products that you are currently using. It's very simple, read the label on the package, it will tell you the name of the company who made it. When you have time sit down and analyze the stocks you want to buy. What could help you along the way is to read some of these financial papers like the *Wall Street Journal* and the *Investors Business Daily*. You will get more information from these two papers than from anywhere. You have to do your homework. The teachers use to give you homework, and if you did your homework you got a better grade on the test.

Even though you didn't like doing the homework it was something that was required. High school got you prepared to do homework and I'm going to get you prepared for life. Read the papers; come up with ideas, but most of all you have to follow the plan, that will ensure your success. It is very important to know that when you use something a million people are using the same product. The supermarket is one way to find stocks. If you watch people filling up their baskets every week, do a little research and follow people around and you'll see they're putting the same products in their baskets every week.

A company makes those products and that is how you'll know which ones to pick for your five companies. You read the two financial papers, educate yourself about the stocks, see if they pay dividends and if you have more than five stocks you are interested in you have to determine which ones you'd like to pick. Be sure to pick the best five.

The other chapters in the book are to guide you through life. The more legitimate investing you do and the more you educate yourself the bigger funds you'll have for investments purposes. Then more money you have in the bank the more money you can put into the five stocks and watch them grow. That doesn't mean you start selling or taking money out. You are a buyer, waiting for your portfolio to grow. Patients are very important in this process. Remember stocks and dividends grow and they split to give you more shares.

When you read these two papers *The Wall Street Journal* and the *Business Investors' Daily*, you will see articles written about specific companies and their new stock options and how the company is doing as far as profits and losses. Companies have a commitment to their shareholder's progress. Read those papers everyday; don't be afraid to ask questions even EINSTEIN asked questions. Reading these papers will provide you with information you need to change a stock, or just follow the progress of the stocks you have in the plan.

I want you to pass this information on to your kids, parents, grandparents and friends. America will get stronger because of this book; our youth will be more knowledgeable. I hope one of you who purchase this book becomes the president, I would enjoy seeing that. Good luck and have a great financial future.

Remember only trust the person in the mirror.